Dear Parents:

Congratulations! Your child is taking the first steps on an exciting journey. The destination? Independent reading!

STEP INTO READING® will help your child get there. The program offers five steps to reading success. Each step includes fun stories and colorful art or photographs. In addition to original fiction and books with favorite characters, there are Step into Reading Non-Fiction Readers, Phonics Readers and Boxed Sets, Sticker Readers, and Comic Readers—a complete literacy program with something to interest every child.

Learning to Read, Step by Step!

Ready to Read **Preschool–Kindergarten**
• big type and easy words • rhyme and rhythm • picture clues
For children who know the alphabet and are eager to begin reading.

Reading with Help **Preschool–Grade 1**
• basic vocabulary • short sentences • simple stories
For children who recognize familiar words and sound out new words with help.

Reading on Your Own **Grades 1–3**
• engaging characters • easy-to-follow plots • popular topics
For children who are ready to read on their own.

Reading Paragraphs **Grades 2–3**
• challenging vocabulary • short paragraphs • exciting stories
For newly independent readers who read simple sentences with confidence.

Ready for Chapters **Grades 2–4**
• chapters • longer paragraphs • full-color art
For children who want to take the plunge into chapter books but still like colorful pictures.

STEP INTO READING® is designed to give every child a successful reading experience. The grade levels are only guides; children will progress through the steps at their own speed, developing confidence in their reading.

Remember, a lifetime love of reading starts with a single step!

Published in the United States by Random House Children's Books, a division of Penguin Random House LLC, 1745 Broadway, New York, NY 10019, and in Canada by Penguin Random House Canada Limited, Toronto, in conjunction with Disney Enterprises, Inc.

Visit us on the Web!
StepIntoReading.com
randomhousekids.com

Educators and librarians, for a variety of teaching tools, visit us at RHTeachersLibrarians.com

ISBN 978-0-7364-3682-3 (trade) — ISBN 978-0-7364-8199-1 (lib. bdg.)
ISBN 978-0-7364-3683-0 (ebook)

Printed in the United States of America 10 9 8 7 6 5 4 3 2 1

Driven to Win!

by Liz Marsham
illustrated by the Disney Storybook Art Team

Random House New York

A new racing season
is here!
Lightning McQueen
takes the lead.
His friends race hard.
They have fun, too.

MOTOR SPEEDWAY of the SOUTH
MOTOR SPEEDWAY OF THE SOU
DINOCO
RUSTEZE
95
RUSTEZE
octane Gain
TURBO VITAMINS

Jackson Storm

is a new racer.

Lightning tries

to beat him.

Storm is too fast.

Lightning crashes!

Lightning watches a video
of his crew chief,
Doc Hudson.
Doc had a bad crash
and never raced again.
Lightning does not want
to stop racing.

A business car named Sterling
builds Lightning
a new training center.
Lightning is excited!
He is ready
to start training and racing.

Cruz Ramirez
is Lightning's new trainer.
She will use
the best training system
to make Lightning faster.

But the training system
is hard to use.
Lightning breaks it.

Lightning wants
to train his own way.
He takes Cruz
to the beach.

Cruz sinks
into the sand.
Lightning teaches her how
to race on the beach.

Lightning and Cruz
enter a small race.
They wear disguises.
They do not know the race
is the Thunder Hollow Crazy Eight!

Cars crash into each other.

A school bus named

Miss Fritter chases Cruz.

Lightning and Cruz want

to leave the race!

Lightning says
Cruz is not a real racer.
Cruz is sad.
She wants to leave.

Cruz has always wanted
to be a racer.
Lightning feels bad.
He takes her to
Doc Hudson's track.

Lightning and Cruz
meet some famous cars
who used to race with Doc.
They tell stories about him.
He once flipped
over another racer!

Lightning and Cruz train
with Doc's friends.
They pull heavy trailers.

Every day, they get
faster and stronger.
They have a lot of fun, too.

At the end of their training,
Cruz beats Lightning in a race.
She is faster!

Now it is time
for the big race in Florida.
Lightning is nervous.

Finally, the race begins!
Lightning thinks about Cruz.
Cruz did all the training,
just like Lightning.

Cruz is a great racer.

She just needs a chance.

Lightning goes to the pit.

He has an idea.

Cruz will finish the race!

Ramone paints Cruz.

Lightning will help her.

Cruz feels

excited and nervous.

She joins the race!

Cruz catches up to Storm.

Storm is a bad sport.

He pushes Cruz

into the wall.

Cruz remembers
one of Doc's tricks.
She flips over Storm
and wins the race!

Afterward,
Cruz quits her job
as a trainer.
Everyone is shocked!

Tex Dinoco will sponsor her.

She will be a racer!

Lightning will be

her crew chief.

Cruz and Lightning
get new paint jobs.
Lightning is happy
to race with his friend!